Tonight

Only

Novella

Layla Stevens

Published by The Scilicet Group, LLC
4139 South Nolan Drive
Pearland, Texas 77584

ISBN: 978-1-941839-13-3

Cover design © **Kristy Brown**

Dedication

To my crazy aunt Katherine "Kerry" Hull who always lived with No regrets. I hope you are in heaven and you have made it to the flip flop. I love you and know that you are smiling down from heaven. Thank you for being you. Live, Laugh, & Love.

Acknowledgments:

Patrice Krumm: Thank you from the bottom of my heart, your friendship means the world to me. You truly are One in a Million, and I would not trade you for all the Pink in the World.

To my Kick Ass Street Team: I love you all the pink sparkles in the world.

To my family: Thank you for believing in me

To my amazing Beta readers: Candice Burna Tice, Amy Abendroth, Jenni Crawford, Stephanie Nett, Rhonda Reuther, and all who helped in this journey.

To my Proofreader: Jenni Crawford, may there always be too many commas in all my books. I always add extras just for you.

To all the amazing authors who are part of this boxed set, I am extremely honored to be considered one of you. Thank you for taking a chance with me.

To the love of my life Rhonda Reuther, may our love always endure life's struggles. And may your "issues" always be taken care of. Love you all the red skittles.

To my Mom: Thank you for giving me the love of reading when I was younger. It has inspired me to become who I am today.

And to my amazing Daughter, Thank you for being my number one fan. I love you gumdrops and popsicles.

SC Hutchinson: Thank you for all you do for me. You truly are an amazing friend.

Tonight Only

†Chapter One†

"Every gift from a friend is a wish for your happiness." Richard Bach

~Addyson McNyte~

The ringtone of Meghan Trainor's *All About That Bass* scared the shit out of me. The stillness of my one bedroom loft apartment was shattered by the incessant ringtone.

I love me apartment. The open floor plan with high vaulted ceilings, clean and sleek lines going throughout the entire place, and stainless steel appliances made it seem larger than it really was. The black leather furniture, glass table, and 60-inch TV mounted above the fireplace gave it a Better Home and Gardens feel.

I was preparing for an evening out on the town in celebration of my new job as a police officer in the city of Albuquerque, New Mexico. I recently moved here from Topeka, Kansas, and now my future is looking bright. So bright, everyone around me will need sunglasses.

"Lo!" "Hey, hoe! It's me, Jasmine. What are you doing tonight?"

"Hey bitch, I'm going out to celebrate. I feel the need to cut loose and let my hair down. I haven't felt like a real woman in several months-- more like a woman in drag."

"To celebrate what?" Jaz asked laughing.

"You'll never believe it, but I got the job that I have been training for. I am so feckin' excited! I'm like a kid in the candy store. I've dreamed about being a police officer for years, and now it's finally coming true."

"Feckin' Really. He-he, you crack me up with your word feckin'."

"Bite me, ass. So, I'm going to check out this new bar at the end of Prospect Ave called Bailed Out.

I hear that this is the place to find all the local smexy men; and since I am single and ready to mingle I am going to dance my toned ass off."

"Awesome! I bet you're wearing your black and hot pink eight inch stilettos, huh?"

"Nope, just the sixes tonight. I don't want sore feet tomorrow for my first day at the station."

"Okay, well, I was wondering if you wanted to go with a group of us to the movies. But seeing how you are going out, I may have to talk them into going out with you instead."

"Awe, thanks love bug for the invite and I may catch up with you later, but first I'd really like to scope out this place. I hear they have kick ass drink specials and this may be the only night where I am not so damn tired from working, so I am going to take full advantage."

"No doll, I understand. I'll call everyone and see what the ladies say, and I'll send you a short text when I know what the ladies are wanting to do."

"Great doll face. Talk to you later!"

I pressed the end button and placed my pink phone beside the deep farm sink next to my pink coach purse.

What can I say, I have expensive taste. I splurge on very few items, which consist of purses and shoes! I can walk into a shoe store and have an instant Shoegasm. Some women enjoy spa's and pedicure's, not me, I'd rather spend my money on stuff I can see.

I look at myself in the long mirror and put the finishing touches on my hair and make-up. I stare at my reflection and think to myself, damn the training has really made my body toned in all the right places.

My long, black hair with electric blue highlights cascades down in the back with beautiful bouncy waves, which makes my perfect olive complexion stand out even more. Thanks to great genes from my parents Greek heritage. I don't have to work on my tan.

I apply a touch of bronzer so that my skin would shimmer in the strobe lights causing it to give off a radiant glow. I apply a thin layer of mascara to give my lashes that lush look and make my ocean blue eyes sparkle, and then I go over my plump lips with a nice shade of red lip stain. My mom always said "it was Hooker red." but I love it.

Satisfied with hair and make-up, I stand up and walk over to my overcrowded closet and take out a simple, yet sexy, silver barely there dress. I slide it over my curvaceous body in an attempt to remove the smallest of wrinkles.

I spray some perfume in the air and simply walk through it, not letting the fragrance over power my natural essence. I don't understand why some women feel they have to bathe in perfume, simply spray and glide through.

I take one last look at myself in the full length mirror and grin with satisfaction. I know I am a beautiful woman, some would even say I am conceited, and I am okay with that, I know I look good.

I am a confident woman and know that I have curves in all of the right places. So far not many men can resist my charms—at least none that I know of. Now I'm not saying I'm perfect, because lord knows I have flaws, but in my opinion I look good.

I have not had any intimate encounters in the past year and hell, my vibrator is getting its fair share of love, but tonight I am looking for the real deal. Not that I'm complaining in the least because B.O.B.{battery operated boyfriend} has done what it needs to do, but I want to feel a real man.

I have spent so much time studying for my exams and working out, that my personal life has been placed on the back burner. But Tonight I am going to have some fun.

When I started in the academy, I had it in mind that I would graduate with high rankings in all departments, and guess what, I did!

Out of the 25 people who were in class with me, I was the only female to pass. Hell, I even out scored some of the men.

And I know it chapped their asses that they were beat by a little, short, crazy, Greek woman. I had a big ass grin on my face during graduation because I actually did it. So tonight I am going to live, no regrets!

My hope for the evening is not to find "Mr. Right" but I'm interested in finding "Mr. Right Now." I want a wam bam thank you ma'am type thing tonight.

Tonight I will be like a man, "I will fuck your brains out and then leave you wanting more." I whisper to myself.

I have too much going on career-wise right now and a relationship would totally ruin that. However, the heat pooling between my legs had other ideas.

So, I grab my purse, slip on those six-inch-fuck-me-now stilettos, and head out the door.

I am not what you would consider a very tall woman. That is why the heels are a must, because being the 5'1 lady that I am I have to add something that makes the men pay attention.

My sexy as sin shoes always do the trick, I wear them with everything, and even in training I wore heels. They all thought I was insane, but I feckin' love my heels. They tried to make me wear tennis shoes or boots, but I am a rebel. And when I kicked their ass with heels on it was priceless.

I find that they add the height and command the respect that my attitude normally gives off with half of the effort.

I am determined to have a great night tonight and only a man who knows how to handle himself and how to handle me will do. So let's see what kind of trouble I can get into, or can get into me?

†Chapter Two†

"Be happy for this moment. This moment is your life."Omar Khayyam

~Kalen Drake~

I am what you call a brick house. I work out daily. My body is my temple and I try to treat it right. I' 6'7, have tons of tattoos and I love body piercings.

I fit in easily with the people in New Mexico, because I look like I am of Spanish decent. I have dark hair but I keep it high and tight because I am an ex-marine. I still wear my dog tags daily, just not ready to get rid of them yet.

I was injured in action and received a purple heart because I helped save my whole family of brothers. I did not care that I was hurt, hell I did not even know I was injured till I passed out, and woke up in a base hospital in Germany. And the first words out of my mouth was asking about my men. I did not care about myself. The nurse told me "all survived thanks to me."

I lived my life as a marine for 8 years. I have been deployed more times than I care to remember. So that life is all I know. Once a soldier always a soldier.

I was considered one of the best sharpshooters in the world, and you tend to go where you are needed. I was a gun for hire so to say. I still have flashbacks but so far they are few and far between. When I was given my life back in the form of an honorable discharge, I didn't know what I was going to do. My family thought I'd finally settle down and make some woman my wife, but so far I have not found the one who stole my heart.

I have a nice nest egg saved up, because there was times I did what you call special assignments for the government. I can live the rest of my life and never work again, however,

I have a thing called "I can't sit on my ass syndrome." It's real. I googled it.

Yet, as far as anyone is concerned, that stuff never happened, and I am OK with that. So when I was tired of fishing and relaxing what did I do, yep I went into Law Enforcement. I think I was only off for a couple of months because I was still pulling a few private jobs.

I am an undercover cop in the great city of Albuquerque, New Mexico. I have lived here for a little less than 5 years, but in the five years I have managed to put several women on the notch on my headboard. But the women here are all the same, they want the fairy tale, you know the one, white picket fence, house, and the two point five kids. Yeah not going to happen anytime soon.

So tonight I'm hoping to add someone new. There is a new club called Bailed Out, and I hear that there are always some fly women in there. They are always dressed to kill and smell like heaven. My biggest turn on is a confident woman--one who knows that she is sexy, and one who is not afraid of me because I'm a cop. She needs to be able to stand on her own two feet.

I will be pulled up at the first bar stool within an hour, but first I have to get myself in check.

I go into the bathroom on the first floor of my ranch style home and turn on the scolding, hot shower and make my way in there. When I left the military, I bought this land and built the house myself. I wanted the house to be something to live in forever. It is a multi-level home, but there are no stairs; only a few ramps and an elevator.

As I am in there I think of how excited. I know that there will be some naughty loving going on tonight. I have been called everything from a "stud to God" and have been told I'm "hung like a horse," on several occasions. I love a vocal woman, I love a woman with sexy ass curves. I don't want to break a little woman in half, because I'm not a little guy, matter of fact that couldn't be further from the truth. Truth be told I have a major crush on my dick. He has always held up his end of the shenanigans.

As I am in the shower I think of my latest conquest and how she made my dick hard by her intoxicating scent. Even now I would so give her a round two, and I am not the type to come back for seconds. But for her, I would consider it. Damn she is making me stand at attention, so to prevent from being a one pump chump tonight I take my dick in my hand and imagine that it's her tight snatch fucking me senseless.

In a matter of minutes I am stroking my monster and soon I am clenching my ass muscles as I spill my love juice down the drain. I stand there for a minute to gain my composure, then I step out of the shower and grab a towel and wrap it around my waist. I wipe off the mirror and grab the trimmers to clean up my facial hair. I have a goatee and my chin is pierced. I finish shaving and spray some panty puller cologne on called "Pleasures" and I intend on giving a female a great deal of pleasure tonight.

I walk over to my closet, and I know exactly what I'm going to wear tonight. I grab my dark denim jeans that look worn. I grab my dark shirt and my belt. I grab the Doc Martins off the shelf and get ready.

It don't take long for me to be walking out the door. I grab the black leather jacket off the hook, lock-up, and head to the garage where my pride and joy is currently waiting for me to ride her. I turn the key and the purr of her engine excites me. What can I say? I like the vibrations that I get when I am riding her.

Maybe one day I will get something other than my Harley, but not in the near future. I have no kids and no wife and that is not in my cards. At least not anytime soon.

Before I know it, I am whipping in and out of traffic and the breeze is nice. I love New Mexico, not hot or cold. The view is amazing. The sun has long set but the lights coming off the buildings looks like twinkling lights.

Before long, I am pulling into the parking lot of "Bailed Out" and hear the steady beat of the music that is already playing. It is only half past nine but already there is a good amount of people waiting to get in. I nod my head to the bouncer and he lets me in and I am immediately hit with the smell of booze, sweat, and sex, and oh how I love that smell. This is my night. I will be myself tonight only.

†Chapter Three†

"Life is really simple, but we insist on making it complicated." Confucius

~Addyson~

I pull up to Bailed Out, and I notice this sex on a stick getting off his hog. I have to fan myself, because I have always had a thing for a man on a Harley. This is no ordinary Harley. This one is all chromed out and is still warm. I really should not walk over, but there is something about this bike that is screaming at me.

So I adjust my shoulders, stand straight, adjust the girls and walk towards him. He is placing his helmet on the handle bars, but my cell phone rings and I can't talk to him because it is Jaz.

"Hey hooker, you should see this sex god that got off this bike."

"Well, we will see you in a few, the girls and I decided no movie tonight. We are right around the corner. Wait for us, and we can walk in together."

"OK, but just so you know I will find this gorgeous creature, and I will make him mine tonight."

"Watch your men ladies, Addy has taken claim on some man on a Harley." Jasmine giggles.

Oh no I don't want to claim him, I want to ride him and his Hog. Hell, Jaz I don't even want to know if he is married. This is a one night stand I can handle.

"Addy, I can't believe that just came out your mouth.

"Well suck it up buttercup, because I don't even want to know his name. I just want to love him and leave him. Tonight only I am going to get m...mine, and who cares what happens tomorrow?"

"Girl, just make sure you have him wrap that shit up."

"Yeah no shit, I don't have time for a crying baby and a man that will not even be there. I want kids, but I am in no hurry for the little demons. I am in love with my body and I don't want it wrecked by a snot nosed, screaming kid. Hell no, I am good."

"Geez, Addy, tell us how you really feel." Said Jasmine.

"I mean don't get me wrong. One day, I might, but tonight I want pure unadulterated hard core sex. No regrets and no limitations, just pure fucking joy."

As I am standing there talking to her on the phone, I am dreaming of what I could to do this man. He is gorgeous from what I can see. Long legs that look like they would be fun to be tangled up in. He has this cocky arrogance about him, and I find it sexy as hell. It don't Jaz and the girls long to get here.

"Well, then hells bells let's get inside and start drinking and dancing. So she can go get her freak on."

"Bout damn time! I thought I would die of thirst!" I say laughing

We get to the door and we are all looking sexy as hell and the bouncer lets us right in. I immediately scan the bar for the sex on a stick. But no such luck.

OK ladies, I am going to get a drink, but before I can even finish my sentence they are off on the dance floor. I have to get liquid courage first, so I make a beeline to the bar.

"Hey darlin' what's your damage tonight?" Dawson, the sexy bartender asks.

"I want a sex on the beach, and a double shot of Jose' and keep em' coming. I will leave my card on file and close out at the end of the night.

"Okay darlin' that works for me."

As Dawson is making my drink. I look over at the bar and who do I see? None other than Mr. Harley himself. "Holy shit!" I mumble to myself. But I guess I am not whispering as Mr. Harley is now right beside me.

"Is this seat taken?" he asks.

I shake my head, and he slides in next to me and I can literally hear my heart in my damn chest. I am glad I put on deodorant because I'm sweating like a whore in church.

"Hey there, how are you?"

"I am fine and yourself?"

"Yes dear I can see that you are fine, so how about let's get all the formalities out of the way?"

"How about we go dance. I don't need your name because I am not looking for a relationship. I don't have time for one." I lean over him and inhale his scent. It sends chills up my spine and down into my lady bits.

"If that is what you want babe. So no names, no games right?"

"Oh there can be games, I like it naughty." I wink at him.

"Damn my kind of woman. So let's see your moves on the floor and then I will know if you are worthy of my bed."

"Oh honey, I could tell you that I am worthy but what fun is that?" I ask.

"Well come on, shake ya ass then woman."

And all of a sudden "My Chick Bad" by Ludacris featuring Nicki Minaj comes on. I just start bumping and grinding. I don't even give him time to think. My inner stripper comes out, and I am using him a pole.

Before he knows what is happening, I am pressed against him. I can feel that my moves are turning him on. My ass is moving and I can feel that my dress keeps getting higher and higher, but I don't give a fuck. I know people are starring and normally I would calm it down a little but right now, I want them to see that I have the sexiest man in here tonight.

I hear him let out a groan that sends chills to my lady bits.

"What is the matter love? Like what you see?"

"Babe, we need to go now, my place or yours, because I am going to fuck you seven ways till Sunday."

"Well, I take it I am worthy of your bed, but are you worthy of mine?"

All of a sudden, I get an earth shattering kiss that makes me so wet that I think I am dripping down my legs. I know this makes me look like a hoe, but I don't care. I whisper "My place is only a few blocks away, let's go."

"Do you need to tell your girls that you are leaving?" he whispers in my ear as he is licking down my neck.

"No, they will figure it out when I am gone. Come on. I want to ride your bike." The look of shock is written on his face but he doesn't say anything, just pulls me to the bar. I pay my bill, and before I know it, I am on the back of his bike. I hike my leg and get on the bike. I can tell he likes what he sees. I smile and watch him get on the bike. He starts the engine and the vibrations go straight to my core. I could have an orgasm right here. But I'll wait. I clench my thighs as tight as I can.

†Chapter Four†

"You cannot have a positive life and a negative mind." Joyce Meyer

~Kalen Drake~

Damn she wants to ride on my Harley, this could be bad. Most women are scared shitless of the bike, they call it a death trap, no this chick wants to ride it. So ride it she shall. Before long we are pulling into her apartment and she is off and pulling on me.

"Come on, the ride over has me so fucking hot right now. I could have sex with you right here in front of god and everyone and I would not give a rats ass if the neighbors see." She whispers in my ear.

So I do what any hot blooded male would have done, I lift her up on my lap and I start kissing her neck, slow at first but then when I hear her moans my kissing becomes urgent and I have to taste this woman. I slide my hand up her thigh and reach her silky panties, I feel they are already wet. I move them over to the side so I can reach the hot passage between her legs.

I plunge two fingers in her tight pussy and fuck her with my fingers. My fingers are slick with her sweet nectar.

"Oh my god, Oh my god, please don't stooooooooooppppppppppp. Fucking A." she whispers.

"Which apartment is yours, babe?" I don't even give her a chance to respond before my tongue is assaulting her mouth, her lips are already swollen.

"My apartment is right there. Here are the keys, and the lock is tricky."

I turn the key, and push the door with mine and her weight and it opened. As soon as the door opens, she has my pants undone and my dick out before we hit the floor.

"I love rough sex, so right now I am going to fuck you since you had your way with me on your bike."

This sex goddess has me so fucking hard that I know it won't take much to push me over the edge.

Next thing I know, she is on top of me and already has my dick right at her wet entrance.

This woman is amazing, and she has me in a damn trance. She is on top of me riding my dick like it was meant for her. I feel her dig her nails across my chest. I jump a little when she graces one of my scars. But I don't let her know it's a sensitive spot.

I reach up and grab her waist and pull her down on top of me hard. She lets out this moan that makes my dick harder than it ever has been. She is fucking me, and I am fucking her. Within a few minutes she is speeding up, and it's like she is riding a bull.

She is riding my dick and all of a sudden I feel my balls tighten, and she lets out the sexiest moan I have ever heard in my whole life. This woman will be the death of me.

"Holy Fuck, damn, shit," she stutters.

The sound of a woman, when she orgasms, it's truly the best sound in the world. When a woman can talk dirty to me in bed, it makes me weak in the knees. I have only been with a few that can get my blood boiling. And right now I am about to combust. I may have bitten off more than I can chew with this one. This little vixen very well may be the death of me.

†Chapter Five†

"Trust in dreams, for in them is hidden the gate to eternity." Khalil Gibran

~Addyson~

Practically out of breath I whisper to him, "Come on let's go to the bedroom and see if we can't get more acquainted."

"Fine by me, though I think you found your way around me easy enough."

"Well babe, you have a body that is easy to navigate." We go straight to the bedroom kissing each other the whole way, undressing each other, and leaving a trail of clothes behind.

Mr. Smexy grabs me by the ass and he picks me up, so I wrap my muscular legs around his slim waist. I dig my heels into his ass never breaking our kiss.

I hear a ripping sound and know that my sexy pink panties are now trash, but I don't care it takes him seconds before he is thrusting into me. I am setting a pace of straight, hard core, grudge fucking, and to my surprise he is meeting me thrust for thrust.

He takes a pierced nipple into his mouth and pulls and I let out a load moan. I had no idea that I loved the little bit of pain that this man is giving to my nipples. I whimper "this is what I needed." And at that moment I tremble and climax around his dick.

"This is what I have been craving." He whispers.

We tumble down to the bed, and I continue my relentless rhythm. He is pounding into me with my legs above his shoulders looking down at me,

I can't help but to smile at her and say, "You're a fucking animal, baby." I roll her over and she says, "Baby, you haven't seen anything yet. Darlin', now it's my turn to take you by my pace." He does just that.

I am wild, though I think he may be wilder than I am. Still, I know how to make a man lose his shit. So what do I do? I start rubbing my clit, squeezing, and reach the piercing there and give it a little flick. I find my nipple with my other hand and I pull on that as well.

"Babe, you keep playing with yourself like that and I am going to turn you over and claim your ass."

So without missing a beat, I continue my assault on my clit and it doesn't take long before I am squirting all over him.

"Oh such a naughty girl, I told you what would happen if you kept playing with yourself. Now turn over and let me claim that sweet ass of yours."

Without even thinking what I am doing, I am on all fours. I hear the drawer open and next thing I know there is a cold gel, running down my ass and before I can even whimper a word or complain of any pain, I feel great pleasure with him inching his way into my backdoor.

"Oh my fucking god, you are so tight." He whispers over my shoulder.

I can't even manage an audible sound, just hard moans, because this feels so good that I don't want him to stop. Which he doesn't, he is pounding me like his life is depending on it.

I feel his balls hitting my clit with every thrust. I cry out while reaching yet another orgasm. This makes the fourth of the night while Mr. Smexy has still not even reached one. He's a fucking machine.

Just when I think there is a break and I can breathe, he pulls out of my ass. He wipes himself off, and claims my pussy doggy style. There is no rest because before long, we are in a different position. Soon, I am sitting up and riding him backwards, cowgirl style on his lap. He finally starts to cum, screaming out a slur of cuss words and the only one I hear is "god dammit."

We collapsed on the bed and spoon one another naked as he's rubbing my back with one hand and holding me around my waist with the other, and all of a sudden he asks "are you ready for round two?"

†Chapter Six†

"Obstacles are those things you see when you take your eyes off the goal." – Henry Ford

~Addyson~

I turn my head and smile at him. "Well for you darlin' I think I can go all night long." I hear him chuckle.

This sexy ass man is now laying on top of me, missionary style holding my hands above my head. He starts kissing down my body circling each nipple, and working his way between my breasts.I squirm when he kisses me from hip-bone to hip-bone and licks around the tattoo that I have. It is two guns, one is colored purple where the other is blue, and then there is also a set of wings in the middle of my pelvic area. I shudder as he licks my sensitive tattoo. I just got them two weeks ago when I graduated. I see him studying them but he never asks any questions about my ink.

He then continues his deadly assault on my body by going down my pubic bone before reaching the apex of my thighs where he starts running his tongue through her my dripping wet folds, luckily they are cleanly waxed. He takes his thumb and forefinger and holds the lips open as he starts to suckle on my clit. This is where he takes notice of the piercing and gives it an extra little tug, and it almost sends me over the edge.

This smexy man then takes two of his other fingers and slides them inside of me finding my sweet spot on the front wall of my lady parts, rubbing it at a rapid pace flicking my clit with his tongue.As he suckles, it brings me to an intense double orgasm as soon as he slides his pinky finger into my ass. I pull him up with a naughty grin and push him back on the bed.

Because I love to be naughty and I love control, I shimmy down his body to find his semi erect cock and jerk it once. It doesn't take me long to make him stand at attention with just my hands, but I love to make a man's eyes roll back in his head. So I greedily take his cock in my mouth and just go over the tip of the mushroomed end.I lick the vein that goes down the center and he grabs my head and starts skull fucking me. I don't mind and I open my throat and take him all the way in. I can feel his balls slapping my chin.

It only takes just a few minutes and I have warm, salty cum sliding down my throat. He still has not moved from my mouth and I continue to take in every last drop.

He pulls me up and gives me a kiss that rattles my insides. I have never had a man give me so many orgasms in such a short time. Hell, to be kissed like he knows my mouth, like my mouth was made just for him.

"Babe lets go get in the shower and clean up a little bit." He whispers as he is rubbing my shoulders and kissing my neck

I am completely out of breath and just nod my head.

"Where is the bathroom, Love?" he whispers just at my right ear.

I get up out of my king size bed and walk towards the bathroom, I look over my shoulder and he is watching me. Normally I would not be self-conscious, but right now standing here with nothing on but my birthday suit, I can't help but to try and cover up my body.

"Don't." He says now standing right behind me.

"Don't what?" I say as I am trying to cover up my body with my hands but of course it is not working, because well, I only have two hands and I'm more than two handfuls.

He grabs, my hands and immediately pulls me in front of the large mirror in the bathroom, and says "Look at yourself."

I turn my head because most of the time I think I am the bombshell, but right now in this moment I want nothing more than to run and hide.

"Seriously look. See what I see. You are beautiful, and you have a body to die for. Women pay millions to look like you. Why would you want to hide that? Please look at yourself."

And I look, I look at him running his fingers down my shoulders, to my nipples, down to my belly button. And then I see him take in my tattoos again. When he sees the police symbol, his breath catches.

"What is this?" he asks.

"No questions remember? Tonight we are just two strangers passing in the night. Tomorrow you will go back to your life, and I will move on with mine. We made an agreement that we would not know anything about each other."

"You are right. No questions."

I can see the wheels in his turning, but he doesn't ask any more questions. I don't think I could answer those questions right now anyway. I don't want to tell him the reason I became a cop was to find the low life bastard who killed my twin brother, Athen. He was killed two years ago. My brother had been into drugs for a few years. Well when he all of a sudden moved to New Mexico, I followed. He got into some trouble and was making drug runs for some asshole. When he was done with my brother, he shot him in the back of the head when his back was turned. Piece of shit! But I shake those thoughts out and tell "Mr. Smexy now come on, let's shower, I think I wanna have my way with you again, before you leave." I walk us over to the shower and turn it on the hottest setting, and step in looking over my shoulder, I smirk at him and happen to look down at his package and he is already starting to get hard. I could get used to that, I think to myself.

He turns us around and pushes me into the corner of the shower lifting one leg around his waist and immediately, he is thrusting hard and fast.

"I am sorry, I need to have you now." He moans in her ear.

"You won't hear any complaints from me." I look down his chest and I see a bullet wound. I want to ask a question, but my mind cluster fucked. He is ravishing my body. And I love it.

†Chapter Seven†

"Sometimes the best thing you can do is not think, not wonder, not imagine, and not obsess. Just breathe and have faith that everything will work out for the best." – Unknown

~Kalen Drake~

I look over at her trying to hide, I have no idea why she is fucking beautiful. She is not some bean pole of a woman. She has curves and I could lick every inch of them.

She looks like she would be beautiful pregnant. She has very womanly features, ample breast and a flat stomach that you can tell she works hard on. She has hips that are perfect to hold onto. Her thighs make a man stand attention. Her ass is fucking sexy as hell. She is perfect.

I look down and I see that she has a police symbol on her pelvic bone. I want to know if she lost a loved one to the force, but she said no questions.

I have never wanted to talk to a woman more than I do with her. There is something about her that makes me want to know everything about her, but I know that in the morning I will leave her bed and I will never see her again. Love em and leave em, are my thoughts.

Our night tonight was simply amazing. So one last time tonight and this time, I am going to make love to her.

So I turn off the water and grab a white fluffy towel and wrap her up. Then, I grab one for myself. I pull her out of the bathroom and dry her off with her towel, and now she is standing before me in all her glory. I can't help but stare at her.

"Like what you see."

"Yes mam I do. I'd be a fool not to. You are stunning and have a killer body. Come on let's lay here for a little bit, normally I am not a cuddle type of person but tonight I can make an exception."

"Well, if you insist, but you must know I sleep in the nude."

"Hell yes! Then I may be able to have my way with you one last time, but if not I can say it has been fun."

"I agree it has been a blast, and I will keep my word and not ask any questions. But I will say if you ever find your way in this part of town, feel free to stop by and say hello."

"Will do darlin'." I could tell she would be asleep before long.

Within minutes, her breathing leveled out and I lay there and listen to her sleep. I think to myself what the fuck has this amazing woman done to me. Normally there are no feelings, but tonight with her I want to stake my claim on her. Unfortunately, though we agreed to one night only.

I get up and get my clothes on, look over at her one last time, and walk out the door knowing I will never see her again.

I get home a few minutes later and look at the alarm clock, it's a little after six in the morning, there is no point in going to bed as I have to be up in an hour. So I lay on my bed and think of her. Who is she? I know I could very easily find out who she is, all I would have to do is phone in her address and they would be able to tell me within minutes, but she made the rules and I will obey them.

Next thing I know my alarm clock is going off, and I look over at the alarm clock and it says eight thirty.

Oh Fuck, I am late. So I haul ass out of bed and don't even bother to change clothes as it's just a new rookie coming in today.

I am at the station within minutes and walk through the door at the same time as some female.

"Hey watchhhhhhhhh where you're going" is the last thing I hear before the wind is knocked out of me.

†Chapter Eight†

"You cannot control everything that happens to you; you can only control the way you respond to what happens. In your response is your power." – Unknown

~Addyson~

I wake up to my alarm clock gawking at me. I look over and smell cologne. What the hell? I go to move and my body is sore but nothing that I can't handle. I walk over to my bathroom and glance on the floor and I see two towels laying on my floor.

"Damn how much did I have to drink last night?" I think to myself. I am about to get in the shower when I hear Jazmine's ring tone yelling at me from the other room, so I turn off the water and move to grab my phone.

"Hey Gutterslut, how was it?"

"What are you talking about?"

"Girl don't play dumb, tell me about Mr. Harley. I saw you on the dance floor and next thing I know you were gone."

"I don't remember just yet, I woke up like literally four minutes ago. Give me a recap please?"

"Damn you had like 9 sex on the beaches and 9 shots of Jose' at last time I talked to Dawson. I told him to cut you off then I saw you on the dance floor with Mr. Smexy, and the next thing I know you are gone. So please tell me you got some of that action?"

"Are you fucking kidding me? No of course you are not. Why would I drink so much? Oh my god are you talking about Harley as in the hot as hell guy with the bike?"

"Uh yeah, the one and only. You told us you would be claiming him, so did you? And if you did I hope like hell you wrapped that shit up. I know he was fine and all but damn you don't want something Ajax can't wash off."

"Let me think for a few minutes and I will call you back."

"Okay Hooch, love ya face."

"Love you too babe and I swear I will call you back."

I walk over to my bed and suddenly last night comes crashing back to me. I slept with a man I did not know, and I reach over for the trash can, and there is no wrappers in there. I get down on the floor and look around, nothing. Fuck… Fuck… Fuck I don't have time for this right now, I don't even get in the shower, I throw on my rookie clothes and my black heels and lock my door and head to the station.

As I am in a hurry to get in the door I don't even notice a man standing there, and the next thing I know I am laying on top of him

Hey watcccccccccchhhh out you ASS!

Last night suddenly hit me in the face. Holy shit I just slept with my boss.

The End for NOW!!!

Tonight Only

Connect with Author Layla Stevens

www.tsu.co/Authorlayla/22142148

Instagram @authorlayla

Pintrest authorlayla

Google + Layla Stevens

Pizap Layla.stevens.author@gmail.com

Tumblir @authorlayla

Twitter @authorlayla

Email Layla.Stevens.author@gmail.com

Like page

https://www.facebook.com/pages/Layla-Stevens/697947530238039

Amazon page

http://www.amazon.com/Layla-Stevens/e/B00MRB0TTM/ref=ntt_athr_dp_pel_1

Buy Links Amazon

Us http://www.amazon.com/dp/B00MR3HQZ0

Goodreads

http://www.goodreads.com/book/show/1877384 5-broken-love-and-forever-bound

Plague

My new addiction http://plag.com/app/

I was born in Tulsa, Oklahoma but moved to
Pensacola, Florida in 1996. I have a huge family
who I shocked them when I told them I was writing
my first book. I have had a love a reading since I
was young. Reading has always been my escape. I
can read and be a princess or a warrior. Reading for
me was always something magical. And I hope to
pass that on to you all.

I am blessed to be the mom of a little girl named Sage who is the light of my life. {I call her Olga, and she hates it} I did not give birth to her but I choose her.

I am blessed with great friends who have always had my back. I have a lot to learn in this world of writing but, so far I am enjoying the ride. I have a fantastic Four that are my true loves. No names will be mentioned as they know who they are. I Love you all very much. {I didn't included alters in that comment}.

I'm very opinionated and have no filter. I speak my mind without thinking of the consequences. Does this get me in Trouble? Yes it does every single day. But I will not change. I march to my own beat. My mom says that I can be a one man band.
I am always willing to help out anyone who is in need all you have to do is ask. I never knew that writing a book would show me so much about myself. I have learned so much in a short amount of time. And I can't wait to learn more.

This past year has truly blessed me in so many ways. I was nominated on several blogs for best LBGT author, and guess what? I won on Coast to Coast Book Besties. Needless to say I'm over the moon excited because I'm firm believer in Equal Rights. So in my books you will find a little bit of everything. I'm not ashamed to step out of the normal cookie cutter box. I like to push the limits, and I love to be different.

"Always remember to let your Faith be bigger than your fear." ~ Layla Stevens

www.ingramcontent.com/pod-product-compliance
Lightning Source LLC
Chambersburg PA
CBHW070651130626
46555CB00006B/2819

* 9 7 8 1 9 4 1 8 3 9 1 3 3 *